The Mummy at Midnight

Steve Brezenoff
AR B.L.: 3.5
Points: 1.0

MG

THE MUMMY AT MIDNIGHT

BY STEVE BREZENOFF
ILLUSTRATED BY TIFFANY PROTHERO

Librarian Reviewer
Marci Peschke
Librarian, Dallas Independent School District
MA Education Reading Specialist, Stephen F. Austin State University
Learning Resources Endorsement, Texas Women's University

Reading Consultant
Elizabeth Stedem
Educator/Consultant, Colorado Springs, CO
MA in Elementary Education, University of Denver, CO

STONE ARCH BOOKS
www.stonearchbooks.com

Shade Books are published by Stone Arch Books
151 Good Counsel Drive, P.O. Box 669
Mankato, Minnesota 56002
www.stonearchbooks.com

Library of Congress Cataloging-in-Publication Data
Brezenoff, Steven.
The Mummy at Midnight / by Steve Brezenoff; illustrated by Tiffany
Prothero.
    p. cm. — (Shade Books)
    ISBN 978-1-4342-0797-5 (library binding)
    ISBN 978-1-4342-0893-4 (pbk.)
    [1. Horror stories. 2. Mummies—Fiction.] I. Prothero, Tiffany,
ill. II. Title.
PZ7.B7576Mu 2009
[Fic]—dc22   2008008006

Summary: Girls are missing all over town. Can Maya figure out what
happened to them?

Art Director: Heather Kindseth
Graphic Designer: Kay Fraser

1 2 3 4 5 6 13 12 11 10 09 08

Printed in the United States of America

TABLE OF CONTENTS

CHAPTER 1
Jill   5

CHAPTER 2
We Call Her Maya 9

CHAPTER 3
A Coincidence 23

CHAPTER 4
Tonight. 31

CHAPTER 5
The Mummy's Curse 39

CHAPTER 6
Sleepwalker 45

CHAPTER 7
You! 53

CHAPTER 8
A Warning 63

CHAPTER 9
Just Between Us. 69

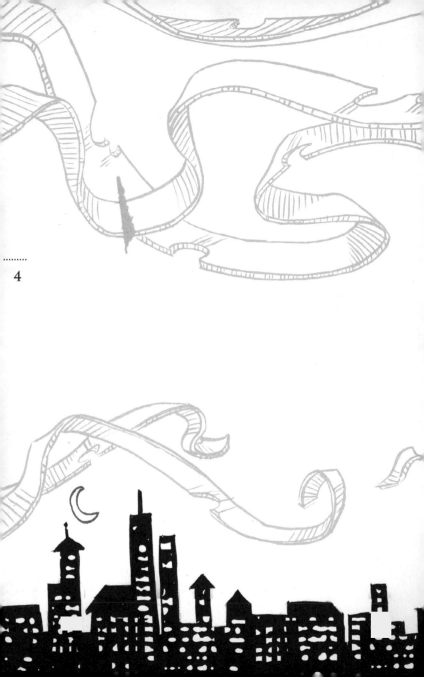

CHAPTER 1

JILL

Jill Conrad rolled over in bed one Saturday night. The alarm clock on the nightstand showed exactly twelve midnight in its big, bright red numbers.

She never opened her eyes, but Jill knew it was midnight. Silently, her bare feet slipped down to the deep carpeting of her bedroom floor.

Jill didn't make a sound on the steps as she went down to the front door.

Her parents didn't even wake up when she unlocked the door. A cold breeze rushed in and sent her long T-shirt flapping, but Jill didn't open her eyes.

She just stepped lightly onto the sidewalk and walked slowly across the yard to the street.

Jill headed for the museum downtown. She walked slowly but surely, as though pulled by a long, invisible rope.

There was no traffic on the Bay Avenue bridge that night. Had there been, someone certainly would have stopped to see why a ten-year-old girl was walking down the sidewalk in her pajamas.

She stopped at the bottom of the stone steps that led to the museum's doors. Then she opened her eyes, but the world was dark.

8

CHAPTER 2

WE CALL HER MAYA

The old school bus hit every pothole on River Boulevard. At least that's how it felt to Maya Naranjo. She rolled her eyes and glanced at her best friend, Will Perez.

"I think the bus driver is trying to make us throw up," said Will.

Maya laughed and looked out the window. The bus was bumping and bouncing beside the river on its way to the Metropolitan History Museum downtown for a class field trip.

There was a big exhibit in town. Their fifth-grade teacher, Mr. Jones, had been very excited about it for weeks, ever since he'd first given Maya and her classmates the permission slips.

Mr. Jones said that the exhibit had never even been in the country before. He told Maya's class that they should all be very proud that their city's museum had been chosen to host the exhibit.

"Did you hear about Jill?" Will asked.

Maya frowned. "Jill the fourth grader? The girl in Ms. Frank's class?" she asked.

"Yeah, her," Will said. "Well, she disappeared the other night."

"Whoa!" replied Maya. "Do they think she ran away?"

"No one knows!" Will said with his eyes wide. "Her parents said she went to bed at the normal time. And I heard on the news that someone drove past the museum at midnight and they thought they saw a girl standing there, but they weren't sure."

"That is so creepy. What's going to happen?" Maya asked.

Will shrugged. "I don't know," he said.

Finally, the bus pulled up in front of the museum. All the students piled out.

"Come on, everyone," said Mr. Jones. He was smiling and clapping his hands over his head to get the class's attention. "Please stay close to me as we go in!" The class gathered around him.

Maya and Will stood toward the back of the group. They looked up at the building.

The museum was big and old. It had a stone staircase and columns in the front.

"It looks like the post office," said Will. "This is going to be so boring."

"I know," Maya agreed. "Another boring day in the old, dusty museum."

"Okay, class," Mr. Jones announced. "Follow me up the steps and inside, and we'll meet Ms. Hill, the tour guide."

Maya and Will stomped up the steps with the others.

Ms. Hill was an old woman with blue hair and funny glasses that reminded Maya of a cat. She'd been the tour guide at the museum forever, or at least for as long as Maya and her class had been visiting the museum. They'd gone every year since kindergarten.

"You kids are in for a real treat this year," Ms. Hill said. "The Metropolitan History Museum is very proud to be the first host in the country of a new and exciting exhibit: The Mayan Mummy!"

A few kids oohed and aahed. Even Maya raised her eyebrows at the word "mummy."

Will turned to Maya with a smile and said, "Awesome!"

The group followed Ms. Hill and Mr. Jones through the huge front hall. The sound of squeaking sneakers on the hard tile floors echoed as the class passed the local history room, the Native Americans exhibit, and the caveman displays.

Maya glanced at the exhibits as they walked past. The fake cavemen were covered in dust.

One of the saber-toothed cats was missing a saber tooth. Nothing was different from the last time they'd been there.

"So far, so boring," whispered Will.

Mr. Jones turned to look at Maya and Will with a frown on his face.

Maya elbowed him. "Shh!" she said. "You'll get us in trouble."

Will just rolled his eyes at her. "Okay, whatever," he whispered back.

"Here we are, kids," said Ms. Hill. The class stepped through a huge wooden archway that was painted gold and red.

They found themselves standing in a big chamber. The room was as high as the whole museum, three stories, and the ceiling was a big golden dome.

In the doorway stood a frowning security guard. Everyone walked past him into the room.

Will made a low whistle. "Wow," he said. "This room is really cool!"

"You can say that again," replied Maya.

The whole class spread out into the chamber. All along the walls were glass cases full of ancient jewels, bones, and weapons.

Mr. Jones stepped up behind Maya and Will.

"Pretty cool, huh?" Mr. Jones said. "They've had this hall closed for years. It was being fixed up."

"This is really nice, Mr. Jones!" Maya said. Will nodded.

"Ms. Hill told me that this hall is the reason the mummy exhibit is here," Mr. Jones explained, smiling. "The people who discovered the treasures thought this was the only hall good enough for them."

Ms. Hill clapped her hands. The class and Mr. Jones gathered around her.

"The Mayan civilization was the only civilization in the Americas to have a written language before Christopher Columbus arrived," said Ms. Hill. She was standing by a case of stone slabs with funny little pictures carved in them. The pictures looked almost like letters.

"That stuff looks Egyptian," said Will.

Maya nodded. The rest of the class stayed gathered around the case. Maya turned around.

She spotted a large glass case all by itself in the center of the huge room.

While the rest of the class listened to Ms. Hill talk, Maya wandered toward the case.

She peered over the edge into the case. A small body was lying there, wrapped in yellowed and torn bandages.

Of course, Maya knew right away what the body was. It was a mummy. The head wrapping was damaged. Maya thought she could even see the person's face.

For a moment, she thought it was a little girl. She leaned over the case to try to get a closer look.

Yup, she thought, *that's definitely a girl. But she's not really that little. She's about my age, I think.*

Then, as Maya was staring into the girl's face, the mummy's empty eyes started to glow. The eyes glowed just a little at first. Then they started to get brighter and brighter.

Suddenly, the mummy's eyes flashed, like a camera had gone off. Then they were empty again.

"So, you've found our little Mayan princess," a man's voice said.

Maya jumped. The security guard had stepped up right behind her. "Oh," Maya said. "I guess so."

"We call her Maya," said the guard.

Maya blushed a little. She looked up at the guard's face as he leaned close to her and smiled.

The man's teeth were yellow and brown, and his skin was rough-looking, like leather.

"Maya is my name," Maya said.

"Oh, is it?" the guard said. Then he laughed very quietly. It was almost like a cough. "Perhaps she's finally found her true best friend. You!"

Maya just stood there. Suddenly, someone grabbed her elbow. It was Will. "Are you coming?" he asked. "We're all going into the movie theater to learn about the dig when they found all this stuff."

The guard stood up straight and looked around, then started to wander off.

"Yeah," said Maya. "I'm coming. But wait till I tell you about what that mummy just did."

Maya and Will huddled in the back of the theater so they could talk. Maya whispered the story of finding the mummy, its glowing eyes, and the weird security guard. Will didn't seem that impressed. In fact, he was paying more attention to the movie than to Maya.

After the museum tour was over, the students got back onto the bus. "I'm telling you, Will," said Maya. "That mummy is . . . I don't know, alive, or something."

"Mmhm," muttered Will. He unwrapped a chocolate bar he'd pulled out of his backpack. "Boooo! Very scary."

Maya just crossed her arms and turned to look out the window. *I know what I saw*, she thought. *Forget Will*.

CHAPTER 3

A COINCIDENCE

That night, Maya hardly slept. All night, she was tossing and turning. She woke up every hour, scared from bad dreams.

All the dreams were the same. In them, Ms. Hill was leading Maya into the mummy's chamber at the museum.

As they'd walk in, the mummy would suddenly sit up and climb out of the case. Maya would scream and try to run, but Ms. Hill would block the door.

In an instant, the mummy would grab Maya. Its small, bandaged hands would hold on to her. Ms. Hill would laugh, and then Maya would wake up.

It seemed to Maya that she had the dream a hundred times that night. So when the sun finally rose and she heard her mother downstairs, Maya was happy to get out of bed.

When Maya walked into the kitchen, her mom said, "Good morning, dear." She put down the newspaper and went to pour Maya some apple juice.

"Good morning, Mom," said Maya, yawning. Then she noticed the cover of the newspaper. The headline read, "Two More Local Girls Disappear." A chill ran down Maya's spine.

"Mom, did you see this?" said Maya.

"Oh, yes," said her mom. "It's horrible. I can't believe it. I want you to be very careful, honey. Go to school and come straight home afterward."

* * *

Later that day, Maya told Will what she'd seen in the paper.

"I know," he said. "My dad told me about it this morning. Creepy, huh?"

"It's so scary," said Maya. "Why would three girls disappear in three nights?"

Will shrugged. "I have no idea," he said. "It's probably a coincidence." Then he looked closer at Maya. "You aren't scared, are you?" he asked. "I'm sure you won't disappear too!"

Maya rolled her eyes. "No," she said.

But something weird is going on, she thought. *There has to be some reason for this happening.*

Then Mr. Jones walked in. Maya turned back around to face the front of the classroom.

That afternoon, Mr. Jones had brought in some photos. One of the pictures showed a big pyramid. It wasn't like photos of other pyramids that Maya had seen. Instead of being kind of smooth on all four sides, it had steps up the front and a flat top.

"The mummy that we saw at the museum yesterday was found in a pyramid like this," said Mr. Jones. "The experts at the museum told me she was only a girl. She was probably about your age."

Maya raised her hand. Mr. Jones pointed to her.

"Yes, Maya?" he asked.

"The security guard told me that they call the mummy Maya," she said. "Is that true, or was he making fun of me?"

"No, he wasn't making fun of you," said Mr. Jones. "That is true. She came from Maya, where the Mayan people lived. Nowadays, we know Maya as the southern part of Mexico, and parts of Central America. Anyway, it must have seemed like a good name for her."

Well, that makes sense, thought Maya. *I guess it was just a coincidence.*

Mr. Jones suddenly added, "That's funny. I don't remember seeing a security guard near the mummy at the museum."

Maya frowned. "You didn't?" she asked. "He was standing by the mummy case."

"I didn't see anyone," Mr. Jones said.

Everyone in Maya's class shook their heads. No one else had seen the man either.

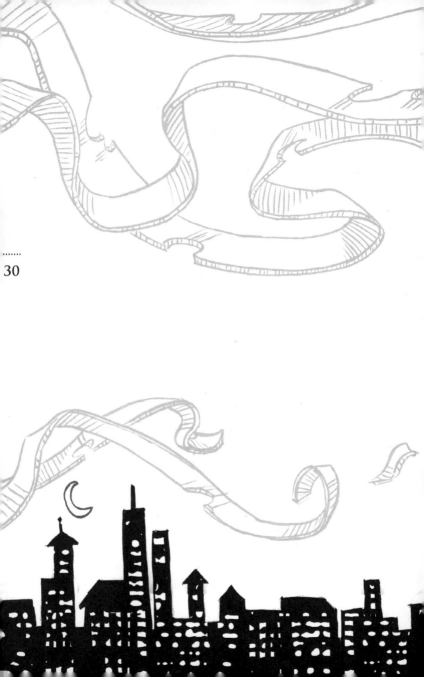

CHAPTER 4

TONIGHT

After school that day, Maya and Will stood together waiting for the bus home. A sixth-grade girl named Polly, who neither of them knew very well, was also waiting for the bus. She looked very sad.

"Polly?" said Maya. "Are you okay?"

Polly turned slowly to Maya. She looked like she was in a trance. "Oh, hi, Maya," she said. "I'm just sad about Beth and Allison."

"The girls who disappeared?" Maya asked.

Polly nodded sadly.

"Are they friends of yours?" asked Will.

"Yes, my very best friends," replied Polly. "They never would have run away."

"Do you know what happened to them?" asked Maya. "I heard that it was just like what happened to Jill. They went to bed as usual. And people keep saying that they saw girls standing outside the museum. Do you think they snuck out or something?"

Polly shook her head. "No," she said. "They didn't mention anything to me about sneaking out at midnight. I hadn't even talked to them since we got back from the museum the day before."

"The museum?" said Will. He frowned. Then he asked, "Wait a second. Did your grade go to the museum this week too?"

"Yup," said Polly. "We went the day before yesterday. Monday. Allison and Beth were both acting so weird when we left."

"What do you mean?" asked Maya. "What were they doing?"

"Well," replied Polly, "I saw them over by the glass case, the one with the mummy in it. I was about to go over and look with them, but suddenly this weird old guy in a dark suit was standing with them."

Polly shivered. Then she said, "That guy seemed really creepy. I didn't want to go anywhere near him. So I just turned around and went back to the rest of the class." She looked down at the ground.

"That must be the security guard you saw, Maya," said Will.

"Security guard?" said Polly. "He could have been a security guard, I guess, but I don't think so. I didn't see a badge or anything like that."

When Maya thought about it, she realized that she hadn't seen a badge either. "Do you know when the fourth graders went to the museum?" she asked.

Polly thought for a moment. "Yeah," she said. "My little brother went on Friday with his whole class."

Maya turned to Will and whispered, "That means Jill Conrad must have gone to the museum on Friday too." Will frowned.

"Then she disappeared on Saturday night!" said Maya.

Will opened his mouth, but didn't say anything. Then he scratched his head. "So what?" he asked. "What are you trying to say?"

Maya didn't answer him. She just kept talking. "And then Allison and Beth went on Monday. They disappeared on Tuesday night!" said Maya. She was practically screaming.

Will opened his eyes wide. "Wait a second," he said. "What are you saying, Maya? What do you mean?"

Maya said, "I mean, everyone who disappeared had gone to the mummy exhibit the day before. And I bet they all stared at that creepy mummy too! That means one thing. Will! Do you know what that means?" she yelled.

"I think so, Maya," Will said. "That means that you . . ."

Maya nodded. She felt dizzy. Then she exclaimed, "I'm going to be the next one to disappear! Tonight!"

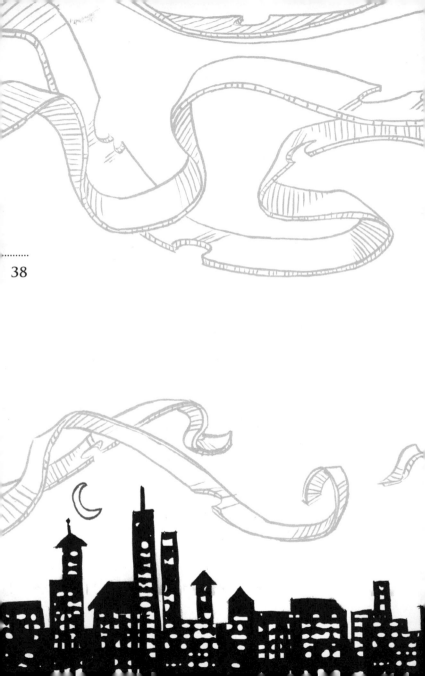

CHAPTER 5

THE MUMMY'S CURSE

"That's crazy, Maya," said Will when they were seated in the last row of the bus. He added, "Why would you run away? It doesn't make sense."

"I'm pretty sure they didn't run away, and I'm not going to either," said Maya. "But Allison and Beth were up close with that creepy mummy, and I bet Jill was too. That mummy put some kind of spell on them. Haven't you ever heard of the mummy's curse?"

"My dad yells at me when I curse," said Will.

"Not that kind of curse," said Maya. "It means that anyone who sees the mummy will get hurt or something. I guess because the mummy is so angry about being a mummy, it makes other people angry too."

Will thought about it for a minute. "So you think the curse is to make girls get out of bed and walk to the museum in the middle of the night?" He rolled his eyes.

Maya shrugged. "I don't know," she said. "But I do know that I don't want to end up in the paper tomorrow morning!"

"Then don't sleepwalk!" said Will.

"What if it's some kind of trance, like dreaming or something?" Maya whispered.

Suddenly, she felt scared. Maybe she wouldn't be able to control herself. Maybe she would run away, like the other girls had.

"I have an idea!" said Will. "I'll wait outside your house tonight. If you suddenly are in a trance and you start walking out of your house, I'll stop you!"

Maya smiled and said, "Perfect."

* * *

That night, before Maya got into bed, she met Will outside. He walked up carrying a pillow and wearing a backpack.

"Hi," Maya said. "So, you'll just sit right here," she told Will. "And then when I come out, you'll grab me and shake me or do whatever it takes so that I don't make it to the museum. Make sure I wake up!"

"Okay," said Will. He sat down on the step. He'd brought with him a big bottle of juice, three sandwiches, a stack of comic books, a flashlight, and a huge chocolate bar. "I'm all set!" he said.

"I see that," said Maya with a laugh. "Looks like you're set for a few nights!"

"I get hungry when I'm on watch," Will said with a shrug.

Maya yawned. "I guess I should go to bed," she said. "Well, good night!"

Will had already stuffed half a sandwich into his mouth and was thumbing through a comic book. "Mmhm," he said without looking up. "Good night."

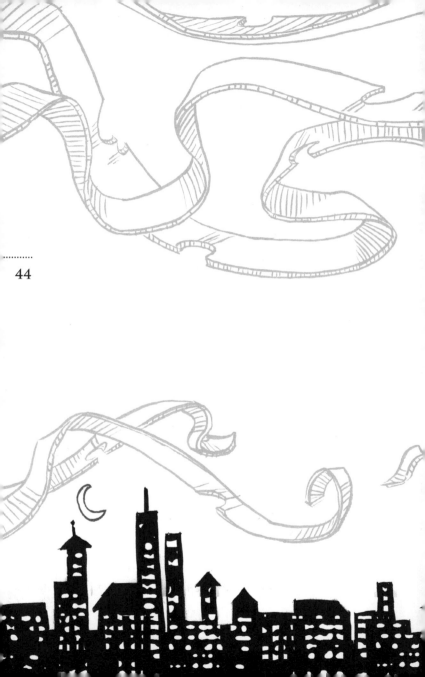

CHAPTER 6

SLEEPWALKER

Maya had a lot of trouble falling asleep. For a couple of hours, she tossed and turned. She tried to keep the thought of the mummy's creepy glowing eyes out of her head.

But whenever she closed her eyes, she'd hear Ms. Hill laughing. She'd see Ms. Hill's scary cat-like glasses. They glowed and twinkled.

Soon the mummy's hands were reaching for her from the darkness.

Maya forced her eyes open. She was still in her bedroom, under her covers. She could see her posters on the walls and her unicorn nightlight next to the door.

She knew if she closed her eyes, Ms. Hill would be back. So would the mummy's hands, grabbing at her. But she was so sleepy!

I can close my eyes for a minute, she thought. *I'll open them again as soon as it gets scary.*

So she did, and Ms. Hill was laughing, and Maya felt the mummy's hands on her shoulders. But this time, her eyes wouldn't open again.

Instead, she slipped her feet off her bed and into her slippers, which were on the furry mat on her floor. Her eyes still closed, she walked out of her bedroom and downstairs toward the front door. Cold wind blew in when she pulled open the door. She walked through and down the front steps.

But she tripped over Will. He'd been asleep, curled up on the steps. Maya fell over him, losing her slippers, and soon they were tangled up together on the sidewalk.

Will jumped up. "Maya!" he shouted.

Maya's eyes started to open. "What?" she asked sleepily.

"Maya," yelled Will, "wake up!"

"Wha . . . where am I?" Maya muttered. Slowly, she stood up.

"You're in front of your house!" replied Will. "I can't believe it! You were actually in a trance!"

Maya shook her head. "That is so creepy!" she said.

"Well, you're okay now," Will said.

"Right. Okay," Maya said. "Let's go."

Will frowned. "Go? Go where?" he asked.

"To the museum," replied Maya. She turned and started walking toward downtown.

"To the museum?" called Will, running to catch up. "It's the middle of the night! Why are we going to the museum? You're not going to disappear, are you?" he asked.

"No," said Maya. She kept walking. "I'm not going to disappear. But I am going to see if anyone — or anything — is there waiting for me to show up!"

"Shouldn't we call the police, or something?" said Will.

"The police? What would we tell them, that an ancient mummy's curse made me walk to the museum in my pajamas?" said Maya.

Will laughed. "Good point," he said.

The two friends walked fast, and soon they arrived at Bay Avenue. The museum was only a block away.

"Wait a second," said Maya. "Can you see anyone over there?"

Will squinted into the darkness. "Nope," he said. "The coast is clear."

"Okay," Maya said. "Let's go."

They slowly walked along Bay Avenue toward the bridge. A cloud moved away from the full moon. Then they could see better. Suddenly, Maya stopped.

"Hold it," she whispered. "Look!" She pointed to the far end of the bridge.

Will could see a figure standing next to a lamppost. "Who is it?" he whispered.

"I have an idea," said Maya. "And it might explain all the weird things that have been happening."

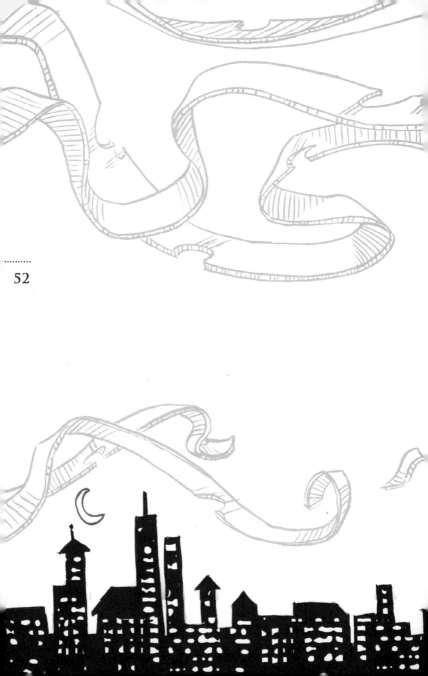

CHAPTER 7

YOU!

Will hid in the bushes at the foot of the bridge. Maya did her best to walk slowly. She kept her eyes closed almost all the way, so that she could see just a sliver of light.

It can't be who I think it is, thought Maya as she walked.

It was hard to walk with her eyes closed. She could hardly see anything. But she had to make it look easy or the person would know she was just pretending to be in a trance.

Finally, she reached the highest part of the bridge. That's when she finally heard the laughter. She could tell it was the figure by the lamppost.

Will was keeping a close eye on Maya. But he was also watching the figure by the lamppost.

At first, the person didn't move. But when Maya walked closer to him, the man slowly stepped out from behind the lamppost.

He started to walk up to Maya. Will stayed low and started walking over the bridge, still watching the man.

Will knew he couldn't get too close, or he would be spotted. They couldn't risk that.

When the person was very close to Maya, Will called out, "Now!"

The man suddenly stopped and turned to face him. Maya had been waiting for Will's call.

She spun quickly and leaped right onto the man. Will ran up and tackled him too. Soon both friends were yelling at the man together.

But he was too strong for them. With a simple toss, he threw them both off him and onto the pavement. Then he stood up.

"I knew it was you!" shouted Maya. The man's leathery face was unmistakable. She remembered that face. It was the security guard from the museum!

"Yes, Maya," he said. "I am the ruler of Chichen Itza!" He towered over Maya and Will. They did their best to back away, but they couldn't get up.

"What do you want from us?!" cried
Will. "Why won't you leave us alone? Why
are you doing this?"

The man glanced at Will and laughed.
"I want nothing from you, little boy,"
he said. His voice boomed. Will leaned
back nervously.

Then the man turned to Maya. He
smiled an evil smile and said, "But I believe
you will be the perfect girl, little Maya."

He reached down for her. His huge,
powerful hands were as leathery as his face.
Maya felt his strong grip on her shoulders
and she shivered.

"Aahh!" the man yelled.

Suddenly he let go of Maya. Once she
was free, she saw that Will had gotten to
his feet and leaped onto the man's back.

Will wrapped his arms around the man's head and scratched at his face.

Maya screamed.

"Run!" yelled Will. He struggled to hang on. "Get help!"

Maya didn't need to be told twice. She knew Will would be okay.

The creepy old man had said it himself: He was after her, not Will.

Maya ran down the bridge toward River Boulevard. As she reached the other side of the bridge, she spotted the museum.

Maybe there'll be someone there, Maya thought quickly. *Maybe there's a real security guard. Someone who can help us or call the police.* She ran toward the museum as fast as she could.

Hoping the doors would be open, Maya ran up the stone steps. But just as she reached the top of the steps, the doors suddenly burst open!

Maya screamed. The museum doors exploded off of their hinges.

Chunks of wood flew out at Maya from the exploding doors. Maya covered her face with her arms.

Then she fell to the ground. She covered her head.

When Maya finally looked up, she saw another figure coming out of the museum. Suddenly, her nightmares had come true.

The mummy girl was walking out of the museum!

Slowly, she made her way to the steps.

Her arms were stretched out. She was reaching for Maya.

Maya screamed again and shut her eyes as tightly as she could. She hoped that she was just having a nightmare.

But when she opened her eyes, she knew she wasn't dreaming. The mummy was heading right for her!

CHAPTER 8

A WARNING

"Oh no!" cried Maya. She turned to run back down the steps, but the creepy man was already running up to them.

"You can't escape from me!" shouted the creepy man.

Maya turned back to the mummy. Its hands were stretched out, reaching toward Maya.

She shrieked. The mummy was almost on top of her.

"Noooo!" Maya yelled. The mummy girl was only inches away. But nothing happened. Instead, the mummy walked right past her.

"You!" shouted the creepy old man at the mummy. "How did you wake up?" he yelled.

The man turned. He started running back down the steps, away from Maya and the mummy girl.

Will had just started walking up the museum steps. As the man ran down the stairs, he almost knocked Will over.

"Watch it!" Will yelled.

The mummy followed the man down the steps. She picked up speed as the man ran faster and faster, trying to get away.

"What's going on?" shouted Maya. "Why is the mummy chasing that guy?"

The mummy suddenly sped up and started chasing the man to the bridge. She caught the man quickly and knocked him to the ground.

Maya ran over to the mummy. Will followed her. The mummy stood over the man, who looked up in fear.

"Why did you save me?" Maya asked the mummy. "We thought you were cursing the girls in this town!"

"No," replied the mummy. Her voice was soft and sweet. "That man was the ruler of my people. He kidnapped me, many years ago. I tried to warn the girls here when I saw him talking to them. I knew he would put them in a trance."

"Warn us?" Maya asked, feeling confused.

"That's right," said the mummy. "I tried to warn you yesterday at the museum, when you looked down into my eyes. Tonight, I realized that was not enough."

"So you broke out of the museum to save me?" asked Maya.

"Yes," replied the mummy. "Now, you two must go."

"Why?" Maya asked. "We could help you."

"The mummy girl just saved our life!" Will said. "Let's get out of here!"

Maya let Will pull her away, but she watched the mummy stand over the old man for another few seconds. Then she turned with Will and ran back home.

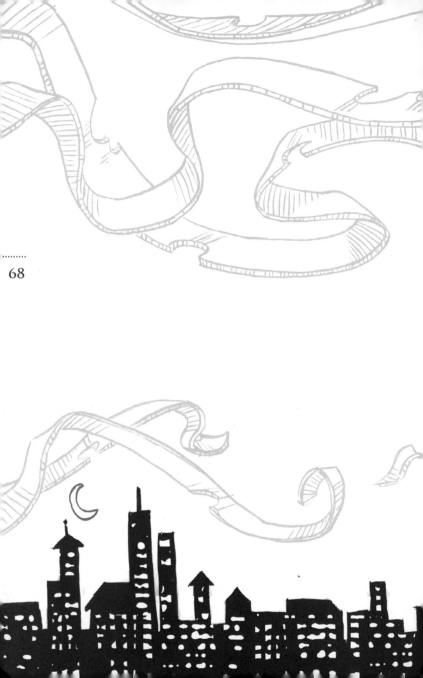

CHAPTER 9

JUST BETWEEN US

The next day, Will and Maya walked to the museum.

"Did you hear about the three girls who disappeared?" asked Will as they walked slowly down the street.

"Yeah," said Maya. "They all showed up at their houses late last night. No one knows where they went. The girls don't remember."

"Yup," said Will. "It's the front-page story in the paper today. There was also a story about someone breaking down the door and smashing the mummy case at the museum."

He glanced over at Maya. "I bet the reporter didn't know the stories were related," he added. He paused. Then he asked, "Do you think we should tell anyone what happened?"

"Oh, right," Maya said, rolling her eyes. "We'll tell everyone that a Mayan ruler put a spell on us to make us walk to the museum in the middle of the night, but then a mummy girl woke up and saved us. Then when he disappeared, the other girls who had been put under a spell finally came back. Good idea."

Will laughed. "Good point," he said. "Let's keep it just between us."

By then, they had reached the museum. They headed down the long hallway toward the mummy display. Some workers had just finished repairing the broken glass. As Will and Maya arrived, the workers took down the "Closed for Repairs" sign and left.

Will and Maya stood over the glass case and looked down at the mummy. But something wasn't right.

"Um, Maya?" Will said. He squinted at the body in the case. "Does this look right to you?"

Maya shook her head slowly. "Is that her?" she muttered.

"That's no mummy princess," Will said. "That's a man."

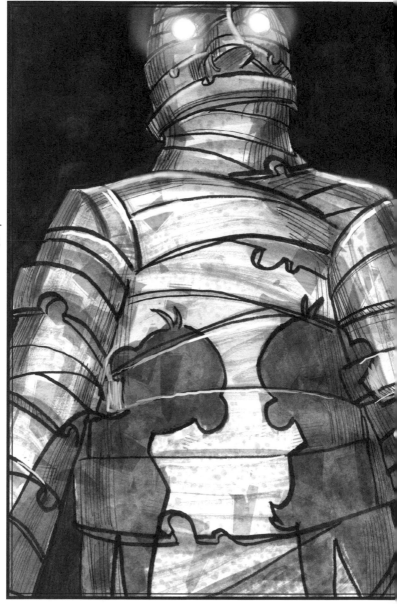

"That's the old man! The ruler of Maya's people!" Maya added in a whisper.

She looked at Will. Will's mouth hung open.

"I guess," Maya said, "she finally got her revenge."

THE END

ABOUT THE AUTHOR

Steve Brezenoff lives in St. Paul, Minnesota
with his wife, Beth, and their small, smelly
dog, Harry. Besides writing books, he enjoys
playing video games, riding his bicycle, and
helping middle-school students to improve
their writing skills. Steve's ideas almost always
come to him in dreams, so he does his best
writing in his pajamas.

ABOUT THE ILLUSTRATOR

Tiffany Prothero is a freelance illustrator in
New York. She graduated from San Francisco's
Academy of Art University, with an emphasis in
book cover illustration. Along with illustrating
for magazines and books, she enjoys taking
care of her feral cats and spending time with
her partner, Mark.

GLOSSARY

ancient (AYN-shunt)—very old

badge (BAJ)—a small sign with a name on it, pinned to someone's clothes

bandages (BAN-dij-iz)—pieces of cloth wrapped around an injury. Mummies are wrapped in bandages.

coincidence (koh-IN-si-duhnss)—a chance happening

exhibit (eg-ZIB-it)—a special show for the public

museum (myoo-ZEE-uhm)—a place where interesting objects of art, history, or science are displayed

pyramid (PEER-uh-mid)—an ancient stone monument

revenge (ri-VENJ)—action that you take to pay someone back for harm that the person has done to you

trance (TRANSS)—if someone is in a trance, he or she is not aware of what's happening

DISCUSSION QUESTIONS

1. Why did the mummy want to get revenge on the creepy old man, the ruler of her people?

2. Who was the mummy in the museum at the end of the book? How do you think he got there?

3. What do you think would happen if girls were disappearing in your town? Would it be scary? How would you react?

WRITING PROMPTS

1. Imagine that you are Maya. Write an entry in your journal about your trip to the museum.

2. Write a short story about the mummy girl. What was her life like when she was alive? What did she like to do? Write about a day in her life.

3. In this book, Maya's class goes to the museum for a field trip. What was the best field trip your class ever went on? Write about it.

MORE SHADE BOOKS!
Take a deep breath and

Jared and his friends thought they were going on a fun camping trip at Eagle Point. But something weird is going on. When they arrive, they find remnants of an awful blaze and a burned cabin. The campground's caretaker seems to be dead, but is he really gone?

step into the shade!

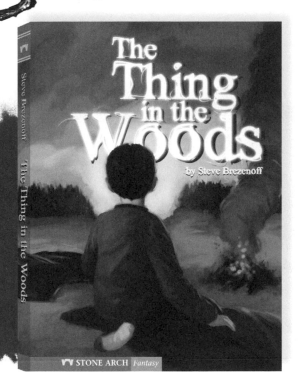

The Thing in the Woods

by Steve Brezenoff

STONE ARCH *Fantasy*

Jason and his dad have car trouble in the desert. They decide to camp overnight. Before they go to sleep, Jason's dad tells him a creepy story. When Jason wakes up, his dad is missing! It seems as though the ghost story is coming true!

INTERNET SITES

Do you want to know more about subjects related to this book? Or are you interested in learning about other topics? Then check out FactHound, a fun, easy way to find Internet sites.

Our investigative staff has already sniffed out great sites for you!

Here's how to use FactHound:

1. Visit *www.facthound.com*

2. Select your grade level.

3. To learn more about subjects related to this book, type in the book's ISBN number: **9781434207975**.

4. Click the **Fetch It** button.

FactHound will fetch the best Internet sites for you!